Helios & Suns Publishers

Jimmy The Big HAT

For Alec, Emily, and Greer.

Foreward

Hello, I am Alec Logan, the son of the author. I was asked to write the forward, so I shall do so now. Ok, I was pretty much there the whole time with "Jimmy the Big Hat". I saw the idea spring to life one day. See, we would go to a bagel shop, Portland Brew, almost every morning. My dad and I would eat breakfast there, and I'd ask him to make up stories.

Now, even before Jimmy the Big Hat, my dad would talk about Theo the Dinosaur and his collection of friends. Screen-time Charlie, who's never off of his iPad. Caliente, the angry chihuahua. These, he would improvise.

One morning, I was expecting another Theo chapter, when my dad broke into a mob voice. He started talking about this crook, Jimmy the Big Hat. He'd made it up on the spot, and he started talking about this gangster always wearing large hats. I like dark humor, so I started laughing immediately.

The next morning, I wanted more of Jimmy, so I asked him to continue. "Make me laugh". Well when he came out with the explosion and the hand landing in the kid's birthday cake, I choked on my food.
"Not that hard!" I said.

He began writing these stories down. Over several months, the story you now have in your hands was created. I hope you folks enjoy this book as much as I do. It's a hell of an idea.

-Alec Logan, aged 12, March, 2022

My name is Vito. I'm going to tell you about my boss.
His name is James Joseph Caravaggio, but everybody calls him
"Jimmy the Big Hat", 'cos he wears big hats all the time.

Always with the hats.

2

One time he wore a sombrero to a funeral.

Sounds funny to you? Nobody laughs at
Jimmy the Big Hat. Nobody.
The sombrero had the tassels and everything.
Not even a snicker.

You never see Jimmy without a hat.

At first, Jimmy didn't wear hats. When he was first getting into the business, he worked for a guy named "Pretty Lucky" Melloni. They called him "Pretty Lucky", since most of the time, bad things didn't happen to him. He'd be on a good streak, then he'd get his hand blown off by a mailbox bomb. Things like that.

Melloni was a real tough guy, a wise guy, and one time, after Jimmy pulled off a job for him, Melloni called him in. He said, "Jimmy, I'm grateful. You do good work, but your head looks like a fuckin' watermelon. Get a hat.

Alphonse Melloni

Get a big hat, or you don't work for me." So Jimmy did. He went real big. It became his thing. And then when he whacked Joey McCann, things started to fall into place for Jimmy.

4

Joey McCann, he was asking for it. Taunting Jimmy, making fun of his hats, and skimming Jimmy's profits. Like Jimmy wasn't gonna find out? Somebody was stealing from him?

Joey was half Italian, half Irish, so he liked to eat at this Italian/Irish restaurant called "O'Gallo's". They combined the food in interesting ways.

Joey was sitting by himself, eating his usual, bangers and ravioli, when Jimmy walked in and fired six bullets into his trachea.

Why all six in the throat? No clue.
Have to ask Jimmy.
It worked.

It's right around this time that "Pretty Lucky" Melloni ran out of luck.

Jimmy now became the boss, and he brought me in to work for him, help him clean up his books, things like that.

Also around this time, Jimmy got a racehorse. Beautiful. He named it "Racketeer". Jimmy thought it had a nice ring to it.

Racketeer was fast. That horse loved to race. So one day at the tracks, Jimmy put down a lot of money on his horse. It was a slam dunk. Jimmy called the othe horses in the race "a glue factory" on account of they make glue out of horses, or so I hear, and that's all the others were good for.

But as it turned out, Skinny Bartollini didn't like Jimmy too much. He also had his own horse, "Concrete Shoes", and he didn't like it being called glue, so he gav Racketeer a little tranquilizer before the race....

Announcer: *"And they're off. In the lead is Racketeer, followed by Sleeping with the Fishes, Capiche, Pushing up Daisies, and trailing is Concrete Shoes. Here comes Capiche on the outside. Racketeer seems to be losing ground. On the inside, it's Concrete Shoes . Concrete Shoes and Capiche, followed by Pushing up Daisies and Sleeping with the Fishes. Racketeer is fading fast! Wait! Racketeer is lying down in the middle of the track. The jockey is pinned under him! It's Concrete Shoes by a length!"*

Anyway, I thought horses slept standing up, but not this horse. It took 'em two hours to get the jockey out. He was OK except for the leg, you know.

So Skinny Bartollini
and Concrete Shoes
won the race, but he
wasn't going to enjoy
the money too long.

Skinny turned up a
week later floating
on the Hudson in
twelve separate
whiskey barrels.

Jimmy has a soft spot too. Sure he whacks a few people, but he likes little dogs. Little yippy dogs. The smaller they are and the more obnoxious they are, the more Jimmy likes 'em. They are always coming back from the groomer with little bows on 'em and shit. You don't like my dogs?", Jimmy always says. "Then shut the hell up and get a golden retriever," and he laughs like he's said something really funny. But he hasn't.

Teasing Jimmy is not a good idea. Jimmy the Big Hat does not like to be teased. If you say anything about his hats, he gets a little smile, then he breaks your kneecaps.

Which puts me in an awkward situation. I'm his right-hand man, his confidant. When he asks me about a hat he's wearing, I mean if he looks, you know, not his best, I need to break it to him easy.

Like this one time, we were at a diner, and Jimmy had this new hat. Gold and pointy and very tall...

"So Vito. I have a new hat."
"I see that, Jimmy. That hat is definitely new."
"You have not told me what you think of it."
"Jimmy, it's, uh...well, you know..."

16

"No, I do not know."

"It's a little… gold."

"A little gold? I look like the fucking Pope? Some flunky from the Vatican?"

"Naw, Jimmy. It's not like that. I just like the 10-gallon fedora a little better. That's all."

"Vito, you're lucky I like you. I don't let nobody else talk to me like that. Now this is a great fucking hat."

"Sure Jimmy. Yeah. Yeah, I see it now."

See, I always gotta do a little dance with Jimmy.

18

Sometimes his big hats could cause a little trouble, like this one time we were at a baseball game and as usual, Jimmy had on a gigantic hat. This thing must have weighed 25 pounds.

The hat was so big, nobody in the seats behind us could see the game. Hell, they couldn't even see the field. Sure enough, guy behind us taps Jimmy on the shoulder, and says something like, "Excuse me sir, I can't see." At which point, Jimmy turns around and points a gun at this guy's forehead."

"Do we have a problem?"

Guy backs off right away. "No problem. No problem at all. All good. Enjoy the game."

Guy was too scared to move, so he sat there listening to the game on his transistor radio. He had one of those earphones in so Jimmy wouldn't hear it.

Jimmy's like that. He has an effect on people.

You know Jimmy Liked little dogs, right? I mentioned this before.

Well, there's an interesting story involving the pet shop where Jimmy bought the dogs. Stop me if I've told you this one. See the people who owned the pet store had to move on account of the landlord doubling their rent. The store was in Jimmy's domain, so Jimmy made sure the landlord got shaken down a little...well, a lot, but at that point it was too late and the Weisenburgs (that's the name of the pet store owners) had to move to a different part of town, Moe Luttz's territory.

The Weisenburgs had barely settled in when Moe Luttz made his grand entrance.

"You got a nice place here. Shame if anything happened to it."

21

Then Moe hit them up for protection money. Give Moe such and such and he doesn't trash the place. So Milt Weisenburg calls Jimmy about it. He's all upset.

Jimmy goes through the fucking roof. And who does he vent to? Me. Vito.

"You hear that? That son of a bitch Luttz is going after the Weisenburgs? They sold me my first Lhasa Apso! And what's this shit about, 'You got a nice place here. Be a shame if anything happened to it.'? That's MY LINE! I say that! Nobody else says that. Vito, can you trademark a threat? Find out!"

"Sure Jimmy. I know a guy at the copyright office. I'll look into it." Jimmy was hot.

"Milt Weisenburg doesn't pay protection money to Moe Luttz. He's a humble, hardworking guy with a family.
He pays protection money to ME!"

I don't think I've ever seen Jimmy that mad before. I was pretty sure Moe Luttz was gonna be taking a dirt nap real soon.

And I was not wrong.

Moe lived in Sands Point. A real nice neighborhood. He drove a '57 Buick Roadmaster, baby blue with a white top. His pride and joy, to coin a phrase. Every time he walked up to the car he'd sing this Buick jingle to himself. It was always on the radio at that time. "Wouldn't you really rather have a Buick, a Buick, a Buick?" You'd always knew Moe was about to drive 'cos he'd sing that stupid fucking song.

Well, Jimmy the Big Hat loaded up that car real good. I think he overdid it, 'cos when Moe turned the key, the car exploded so bad it sent up a mushroom cloud you could see in Jersey.

25

Some poor kid was having a sixth birthday party.

Kids were all sitting outside, tablecloths, party hats, those things you blow into where they shoot out and go back in, whatever the fuck you call those things.

Little Petey was about to blow out the candles when a hand landed in his cake.

I heard he never had another birthday party. It freaked him out.

When Jimmy heard about the kid, he bought Petey 200 shares in the Toucan Casino in Carson City. Never mind the place was losing ten grand a night at the time.
Jimmy can be generous to a fault.

I remember Jimmy would joke about Moe Luttz. "Hey Vito, you hear about the Moe thing? He's all over the neighborhood. Get it?"

Between you and me, Jimmy's a better mobster than he is a comedian.

Now it's about this point that the Feds were starting to close in on Jimmy.

We thought it would be a good idea for him to get away for a while, use an alias, pretend to be someone else. Jimmy picked Santa Barbara. Very nice beach town in Southern California. Beautiful, and pretty much mob free.

He decided to lay low as a camp counselor. Jimmy changed his name to Brice and started wearing regular hats. Truth be told, he didn't look too authentic. Whatever a "Brice" looks like, it ain't Jimmy. Jimmy was 47, with some rolls around the middle, and grey coming through.

The rest of the counselors were, like, 20. He did his best to fake it. The polo shirt, the white shorts. The forced smile on his face. Jimmy wasn't too good at changing his persona, however, surprising as that may sound.

So on the first day of summer camp, a little girl walks up to him and says, "You have a big head." And Jimmy says, "Shut your pie hole, you little shit!"

Every morning, they would gather around for what they called "campfire", only there was no camp, and no fire. They were at Buena Vista Elementary School.

And they'd sing those dumb songs and do cheers and shit that would get stuck in your head all day. And Jimmy, I mean "Brice", would stand in the back with his arms folded and say things like "Jesus" under his breath.

There was this one counselor, Colleen, who really got on Jimmy's last nerve. She had too much energy, real bubbly and perky.

And if there's one thing Jimmy cannot stand, it's perky. At least in some cases.

30

Colleen talked to the kids like they were three years old. Real wide-eyed.

One day she was in front of the group playing this game called, "Guess what I am", which particularly irked Jimmy.

Colleen did something like, "I've got a blue head, large wings, and I like to fly around the garden",

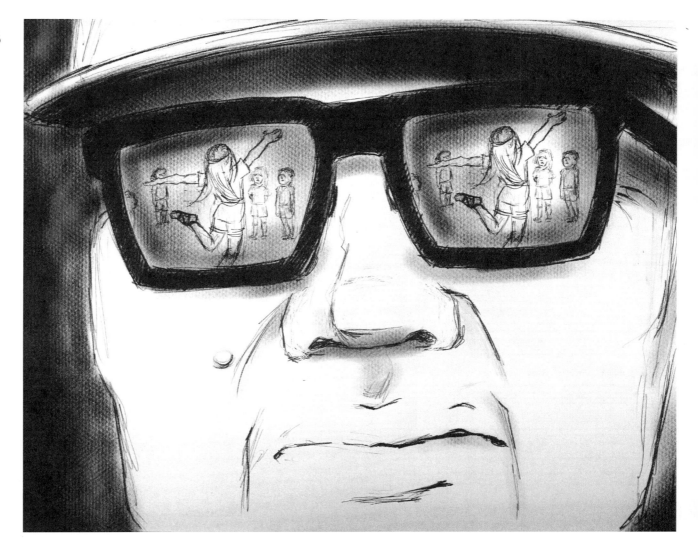

and Colleen started flapping her arms and running around in a circle, and something just snapped in Jimmy.

It wasn't obvious to anybody at the time, just another muttering under his breath. Only this time, he said, "That's it."

It became increasingly apparent that "Brice" was not your ordinary camp counselor. And sometime later, when they were on a field trip, the head counselor had a talk with Jimmy.

"Brice, the other groups are making ice cream."
"And?"
"And you're teaching your kids how to use a garotte."
"It's a life skill."
"Where's Colleen?"
"Where's Colleen? What do you mean, 'Where's Colleen?'"
The counselor said it again. "Brice, where is Colleen?"

So Jimmy points to the middle of the lake. Says nothing.
The head counselor stares at Jimmy.

Jimmy says, "Don't worry about it."

Clearly, Jimmy's tenure as camp counselor had come to an abrupt halt.

Before the police got wind of the goings on at Camp Sesquahappawachie, Jimmy was on a plane to LaGuardia.

Suffice it to say, Jimmy stayed on the down low for a while, to later emerge more "Jimmy the Big Hat" than ever. But these are stories for a later time. We'll talk again real soon.

Cheers, Vito.

As of this writing, Vito Maglione is now living in the federal witness protection program under an assumed (and unabashedly incongruous) name.

Andy Logan is a musician, songwriter and author. He was the lead guitarist and co-lead singer for Geffen recording artists Little America, and has had songs place in the finals or semifinals in International songwriting contests eight times.

He was voted "most humorous" in his senior class, and was once told by a guy he barely knew that he was "flat out hilarious", which earned him (in his eyes) the credentials to write this book. Andy lives in Nashville with his wife Alison, his son Alec, and an African grey parrot named Ella.

Although he has numerous musical recordings to his credit, this is his first book.

Alison Logan is a Canadian born artist and illustrator. She has a BFA in Illustration and has studied with artists Warren Chang, Anthony Rider, and Donato Giancola.

She is a commissioned portrait artist, a member of The Portrait Society of America, and has exhibited in Buffalo, NY, Nashville, TN, and Frankin, TN. Alison has taught art professionally for 15 years. She works in a variety of styles and mediums and enjoys the resulting chaos.

...the birthday, ... but ...
fat and bald ... but ...
everybody he's so ...
I remember Jimmy ... would ... the
about the Moe Letts ... this ... he's all
Vih. You learn about the ... ?"
over the neighborhood. Get ... ta/ker
Between you and me, Jimmy ... about the
mobster than he is a comedia ... Jimmy
Now it's about this point ... he
starting to ... close in ... be a good ... while ...

...shit you pie... Every morning they "camp...
for what they called "camp — and at
that he was no[t] camp — and at Buena Vista elementary schwa...
they were at Buena Vista elementary sc...
And they'd sing these dumb songs and
do cheers and shit that would get
stuck in your head all day. And Jimmy
I mean "price" would stand in the ba...
with his arms folded and say things
"Jesus" under his breath.
...this one counselor, [Colle
...last nerve.
...bubbly a

CPSIA information can be obtained
at www.ICGtesting.com
Printed in the USA
BVRC100826030522
635993BV00008B/154